THE DEATH PENALTY

Is It Justice?

Richard Steins

Twenty-First Century Books

A Division of Henry Holt and Company
New York

Twenty-First Century Books
A division of Henry Holt and Company, Inc.
115 West 18th Street
New York, New York 10011

Henry Holt® and colophon are registered trademarks of Henry Holt and
Company, Inc.
Publishers since 1866

Published in Canada by Fitzhenry & Whiteside Ltd.
91 Granton Drive, Richmond Hill, Ontario L4B 2N5

Printed in Mexico

Created and produced in association with Blackbirch Graphics, Inc.

Library of Congress Cataloging-in-Publication Data

Steins, Richard.
    The death penalty, is it justice? / Richard Steins. — 1st ed.
      p.   cm. — (Issues of our time)
    Includes bibliographical references and index.
    ISBN 0-8050-2571-5 (alk. paper)
    1. Capital punishment—United States—Juvenile literature. I. Title. II. Series.
HV86699.U5S73   1993
364.6'6'0973—dc20   92-34636
                                                                CIP

AC

Contents

■ ■ ■ ■ ■

Introduction

. . . . .

The Execution of Gary Gilmore

The morning of January 17, 1977, was sunny and cold in Utah. At the state prison near Salt Lake City, a 36-year-old prisoner named Gary Mark Gilmore walked into a gray, concrete building on the prison grounds and took a seat in an old leather armchair placed on a low platform. Ten yards in front of the chair was a green canvas sailcloth stretched over a wooden frame. Five small holes, each three feet apart, had been cut in the sailcloth.

On a bench behind the green cloth—and out of Gary Gilmore's view—sat five men. Each one held a .30-caliber Winchester rifle. The holes in the sailcloth had been cut for the rifle barrels. In a matter of minutes, Gary Gilmore would be executed by firing squad for the crime of murder.

The execution of Gary Gilmore in 1977 brought the issue of the death penalty to the forefront of America's ongoing national debate about capital punishment.

A Lonely, Troubled Life

Gilmore had been in trouble with the law from the time he was a teenager. When he was 14, he was arrested for stealing a car. From then until the date of his execution, he was in and out of prison on a number of charges, including robbery, assault, and rape. By the time he was in his mid-thirties, Gilmore had spent half of his life in jail.

In 1976, Gilmore was released from prison on parole. But he was soon in trouble again. Drinking heavily, he went hitchhiking and began to steal. One night, on the spur of the moment, he decided to hold up a gas station. The attendant did not resist, and for no apparent reason, Gilmore shot him to death.

A few days later, Gilmore robbed a motel in Provo, Utah, and murdered the night clerk. As he tried to hide the gun moments after the shooting, it fired accidentally, wounding him in the hand. When he rushed to get medical assistance, Gilmore was arrested. It was the end of the line for Gary Gilmore.

"I Want to Die"

Gilmore's trial lasted only three days. The outcome was never in doubt. Gilmore was convicted of murder and sentenced to death. Under Utah law, he had the choice of dying by firing squad or by hanging. Gilmore chose the firing squad, also the method chosen by 38 of the 44 prisoners before him who had been executed in Utah since it had become a state in 1896.

Gilmore's case soon became known all over the country—for one reason. Unlike almost every other individual sentenced to death in the United States, Gilmore did not wish to fight his conviction. In fact, he insisted that the sentence be carried out as quickly as possible. He said, "I would definitely prefer a quick death to a slow life in the joint."

Often, the appeals process—the legal attempts to get a sentence overturned by taking a case to a higher court or to the governor—takes 5 to 10 years. But Gilmore wanted none of this. When his lawyers appealed the sentence to the Utah Supreme Court, Gilmore fired them. Later, when the governor of Utah postponed the execution in order to review

This artist's original sketch shows how execution by firing squad was carried out in Utah. Five riflemen, four with live ammunition, fired at a hooded Gilmore from behind a dark screen. Only one of the rifles contained blanks, though none of the five executioners knew which one it was.

the case, Gilmore flew into a rage and tried to commit suicide. His mother became involved, as she joined forces with private organizations opposed to the death penalty in order to save her son's life. Through it all, Gilmore kept insisting that he be executed quickly.

The witnesses who saw Gary Gilmore die said he was in a good mood as he took his seat in the old leather armchair on that cold January morning. A prison official then pinned a black bull's-eye to his chest as the warden read the death sentence. With a smile on his face, Gilmore said, "Let's get on with it." At the count of three, the rifles fired. Two minutes later, Gary Gilmore was pronounced dead. His execution was the first in the United States in 10 years.

Questions About the Death Penalty

Gilmore's execution raised a number of important questions that are still being debated today:

• Does a prisoner have the right to die quickly rather than wait for years while the appeals process drags on?

• Why does the appeals process take so long?

• Why, in a time when many countries have abolished the death penalty, does the United States still execute criminals?

• Is the death penalty just, or is it a legalized form of murder?

• Does the death penalty actually prevent crime by frightening potential criminals?

• Is it cruel to kill someone in an electric chair or a gas chamber?

• Is it fair to all Americans that some states have strict death-penalty laws, while others employ long, complicated legal procedures that make it almost impossible for a criminal to be executed?

The death penalty, or capital punishment, as it is often called, has been in practice throughout human history. No matter what the form of government, whether a monarchy, a dictatorship, or a democracy, men and women have been executed for a wide variety of reasons. In ancient times, people were executed for robbery and forgery. In the Middle Ages, they were put to death for teaching doctrines opposed by the Church. And in America only 300 years ago, at least 25 people were executed in Massachusetts for being "witches."

But the methods of execution have changed a great deal over time, and there are fewer crimes today that can lead to execution. Nevertheless, capital punishment is still an important issue for the American people, one that is debated by religious and political leaders and by ordinary people in towns and cities across the country.

1

The Death Penalty Through the Ages

Men and women have been executed for crimes for thousands of years. The first book of the Bible contains a passage about the death penalty: "Who so sheddeth man's blood, by man shall his blood be shed: for in the image of God made he man" (Genesis 9:6). The book of Deuteronomy (19:21) also speaks of severe punishment for anyone committing a crime: "And thine eye shall not pity; but life shall go for life, eye for eye, tooth for tooth, hand for hand, foot for foot." In other words, the Bible says that one should be punished in a way that matches the severity of the crime. If you take someone's life, you must lose your own.

People who are against capital punishment, however, can also quote passages in the Bible to support their position. They point to the fifth

Stoning was a popular form of execution in ancient Rome because it enabled many members of society to take an active part in the punishment of criminals.

commandment in Deuteronomy: "Thou shalt not kill." And in the New Testament, opponents cite the message of Jesus as one of mercy toward criminals as well as the poor.

The Death Penalty in Ancient Times

People may interpret the Bible differently, but it shows clearly that capital punishment existed in ancient times. In the ancient kingdom of Babylonia, in what is now Syria and Iraq, one of the first great sets of laws was written down. Known as the Code of Hammurabi, these laws were named for the Babylonian king, who ruled from about 1792 to 1750 B.C. The Code of Hammurabi contained many specific punishments for different kinds of crimes. For example, a person could be executed for robbery or for committing adultery, as well as for murder. Depending on the crime, one could be beheaded, stoned, or even drowned.

This engraving shows the Babylonian king, Hammurabi, worshiping in front of the sun god. Hammurabi created one of the first written codes of punishment for specific crimes.

In ancient Babylonia, criminals were expected to suffer. Today, our laws are designed not only to punish criminals but also to offer them the opportunity to reform.

Three criminals hang from wooden crucifixes as punishment for their crimes in ancient Rome.

In ancient Rome, one common form of execution was crucifixion—hanging from a wooden cross. This practice may have begun in Carthage, in North Africa, and the Romans probably borrowed it from the time they occupied Carthage. Crucifixion was used frequently in civil wars and especially to put down Jewish opposition in Palestine, then under Roman occupation.

It was common practice among the Romans to force the prisoner to carry the cross to the place of execution. The prisoner would then be either nailed or tied to the cross, and the legs were often broken in order to cause more pain. A person on a cross dies either of suffocation, brought on by the strain of hanging, or of starvation. To instill fear among the people, the Romans would often leave the body on the cross, its eyes eaten by birds and its flesh rotting in the sun.

Jesus Christ, who was sentenced to death by the Romans, is the best-known figure to be executed by crucifixion. Once a symbol of the lowest form of criminal death, the cross is now the principal holy symbol of Christianity.

Another form of execution in Roman times was stoning. In the fourth century A.D., a 13-year-old girl named Agnes was sentenced to death by stoning after refusing the offer of marriage from a wealthy older man. Today, Agnes is a saint of the Roman Catholic Church. During the age in which she lived, women were often stoned to death if they violated the marriage customs of the times.

The Death Penalty in the Middle Ages During the Middle Ages, capital punishment began to be administered by the Church. As the Roman Empire collapsed, the Christian Church took on many responsibilities of government. Where Roman governors once ruled, bishops came into power. The Church owned vast amounts of land. It fed people and tended to their spiritual needs. Since the death penalty had been around for centuries, it fell to the Church to take on the responsibility for its administration.

In 1233, Pope Gregory IX established the Inquisition, a kind of court to suppress heresy—that is, beliefs that the Church considered a violation of its teachings. Torture was permitted in the questioning of suspects, and most trials ended with a guilty verdict. If a person refused to confess, burning at the stake was thought to be a fitting punishment. A person who was burned at the stake was tied to a wooden pole. Dried wood and leaves were then scattered about his or her feet and ignited.

In 1478, another inquisition was established by King Ferdinand and Queen Isabella of Spain. This inquisition was under the control of the Spanish state, and its purpose was to persecute Jews and Muslims living in Spain who had not converted to Christianity. The Spanish Inquisition was much more severe than the earlier

"Nontraditional" forms of capital punishment have been devised by different cultures through the centuries. In India, during the 1800s and early 1900s, elephants were trained to take part in executions. With this method, the criminal's hands were tied behind his or her back, and the person's head was laid on a stone block. Then, with one stamp of its giant foot, the elephant would crush the victim's head.

A common form of punishment during the Middle Ages in Europe was burying people alive. With this method, criminals were bound and thrown into open graves, where they were covered over with dirt. Death by suffocation soon followed.

inquisition and was opposed by the pope. The grand inquisitor, Tomás de Torquemada, became a figure of terror throughout Spain. In 1492, Jews and Muslims were expelled from Spain, but by this time, the Inquisition had been extended to all aspects of people's lives. One of its most terrifying moments was the auto-da-fé, a ritual mass burning at the stake.

The Death Penalty in Early England and France

The death penalty was not reserved for common criminals or for those opposing religious beliefs. Kings and queens could also be executed for political reasons. Some of the most famous political executions in

English history were the beheadings of three queens—Anne Boleyn and Catherine Howard, wives of King Henry VIII (1491–1547), and Mary Queen of Scots. Anne Boleyn, second wife of Henry VIII, was accused of adultery and of being a witch and was beheaded in 1536. Henry's fifth wife, Catherine Howard, was accused of "immoral behavior" and was beheaded by a swordsman in 1542. Mary Queen of Scots, also known as Mary Stuart, was accused of plotting to kill Queen Elizabeth I of England and was beheaded in 1587.

Anne Boleyn, the second wife of England's Henry VIII, was beheaded for allegedly being a witch and for committing supposed acts of adultery.

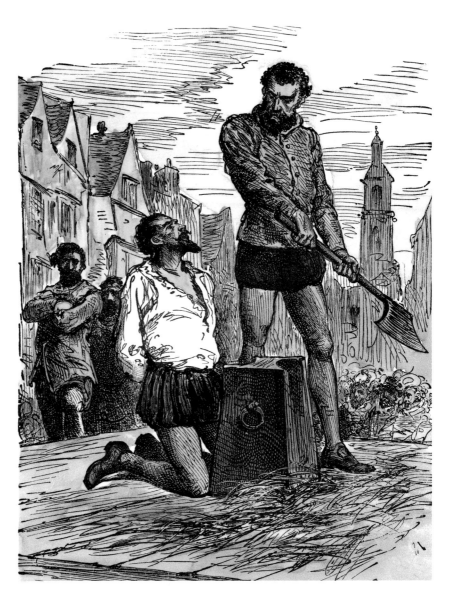

In the early 1400s, public beheadings became a form of punishment for nobles and a popular entertainment for the masses in France and England.

None of these three queens was really executed for the reasons given; they were simply victims of politics. Their behavior was considered treasonous, and the punishment for treason was death.

Execution by a swordsman was thought to be worthy of a noble person. Lowly criminals were hanged or drawn and quartered (tied to horses and then torn apart as the horses pulled in opposite directions). As a reminder of what awaited anyone who broke the law, the heads of common criminals were placed on stakes and displayed on bridges over the Thames River in London.

In early France, burning at the stake and beheading by guillotine were the most common forms of execution. Joan of Arc, the French national heroine and Catholic saint, had tried to help the heir to the French throne rid the country of the English, who were occupying parts of France. She was captured by English soldiers and turned over to French Church officials who supported the English. She was tried for heresy and witchcraft and burned at the stake on May 30, 1431.

But most French prisoners—whether common people or the nobility—suffered the death penalty by guillotine. The victim would lie face down, his or her neck held in place by a wooden brace. High above was a sharp blade, which, when released, would fall swiftly, cutting the victim's head off.

During a period of the French Revolution known as the Reign of Terror (1793–1794) thousands of men and women were beheaded in executions carried out before cheering crowds. The government at the time was a dictatorship. It passed laws making many crimes "treason," and thus punishable

A man's head is placed inside the wooden yoke of a guillotine just before his execution.

by death. An ordinary person, for example, could go to the guillotine for hoarding food. Members of the nobility were executed just because they were from the old ruling class. The guillotine's most famous victims were the deposed king and queen, Louis XVI and Marie Antoinette.

Movements to
Abolish the Death Penalty
Death as punishment for crimes continued to grow in popularity in Europe during the late 1700s. In England at the beginning of the 1800s, more than 200 crimes were punishable by the death penalty.

Gradually, movements to abolish the death penalty began to appear. The modern movement to end the death penalty began in the 1700s with the writings of French philosophers Montesquieu (1689–1755) and Voltaire (1694–1778). Both men were concerned with preserving individual liberties from attacks by government. The death penalty, they believed, was a violation of a person's basic rights as a human being.

Another strong opponent of capital punishment was the Italian criminologist and jurist Cesare Beccaria (1738–1794). His *Essay on Crimes and Punishments*, published in 1764, was one of the first arguments against the death penalty and the inhumane treatment of criminals.

In the 1700s, French philosophers Montesquieu (*above, left*) and Voltaire (*above, right*) began the earliest-known movement to abolish the death penalty. They believed that capital punishment violated basic personal liberties that should be protected by the government.

In England, the philosopher Jeremy Bentham (1748–1832) worked tirelessly to have the number of crimes carrying the death penalty reduced. He was one of the first English reformers who began a movement that finally led to the abolition of the death penalty in England in the twentieth century.

These early opponents of the death penalty helped define the key moral and ethical issues surrounding capital punishment. As they introduced the concepts of basic human rights and questioned inhumane treatment, these philosophers and jurists set the stage for a continuing debate.

2

.....

The Death Penalty in U.S. History

The first colonists from England landed in what is now Virginia, at Jamestown, in 1607. They brought with them English laws, customs, and traditions. In the United States today, the death penalty is used only in the most extreme and horrible cases of murder. During the time of the first colonists, however, a criminal could be sentenced to death for 150 different crimes. Included among those crimes were robbery, counterfeiting, witchcraft, arson, slave rebellion, and even some forms of lying.

Death was usually by hanging. Since most documents from this time have not survived, it is difficult to say who the first colonist to be executed was. One of the earliest records is of a man named Frank, who was executed in Virginia in 1622 for stealing a calf.

Although hanging was the most common form of capital punishment in colonial America, many slaves were publicly burned for their crimes.

Death by hanging can be slow and painful. If the victim's neck does not break immediately, he or she will slowly suffocate while dangling at the end of the rope. In colonial America, hanging often took place by making a condemned person climb up a ladder with a noose around his or her neck. After the other end of the rope was tied to the branch of a tree, the ladder would be kicked away. In other cases, the noosed criminal would stand in a cart beneath the branch of a tree. The cart would then be driven away, and the person would hang.

The Puritans and the Death Penalty

The Puritans came to New England in the 1620s to escape religious persecution in England. They were not tolerant of others with different religious beliefs. When Quakers began to move into Massachusetts in the 1650s, the Puritans tried to drive them out. Some Quakers had their tongues pierced with hot irons and were expelled from the colony. They were threatened with hanging if they returned.

In spite of the dangers, many Quakers continued to move to New England. In 1659, three Quaker missionaries were sentenced to be hanged at Boston Common. One of them, Mary Dyer, had already climbed the ladder, when she received a last-minute pardon from the governor of the colony.

After her pardon, Mary Dyer was expelled from Massachusetts, but in 1660 she returned. Once again, she was sentenced to death. As she stood on the ladder, she was offered another pardon if she would leave the colony. She refused, and the ladder was kicked from under her.

The execution of Mary Dyer is remembered today by a statue of her that stands in Boston Common. The execution of Quakers disturbed the English king, Charles II. Even though he disliked Quakers, he ordered the executions to stop. From that point on, the Puritans ended the execution of Quakers, but they would still beat them in public and expel them from Massachusetts.

The Salem
Witch Trials
One of the most famous episodes in American history occurred in Salem, Massachusetts, in 1692. At that time, at least 25 men and women were hanged for witchcraft. The death penalty for witchcraft was common throughout Europe. Many people of the time believed in the power of the dcvil to possess human beings. Possessed people were considered witches who had the power to cast spells on others, making them ill or insane.

In England, over a period of several hundred years, more than 30,000 men, women, and children were executed for witchcraft. The episode in Salem

In 1692, hysteria over witchcraft gripped the Massachussetts colony. In Salem alone, 25 men and women were hanged for supposedly practicing witchcraft. Many of those executed were members of the church, such as the Reverend Stephen Burroughs, shown here.

was insignificant by comparison, but it was a tragic moment in our country's early history. Contrary to popular belief, the men and women condemned at the Salem witch trials were *not* executed by burning at the stake, but by hanging.

It all began when two young girls, 9-year-old Elizabeth Parris and her 11-year-old cousin, Abigail Williams, began acting as if they were possessed by evil spirits. The girls said that they were being tormented by witches and began to accuse a number of their neighbors of being in league with the devil. In a short time, about 47 people had been accused. Some of them confessed to being witches. Anyone who admitted to being a witch was not executed. Those who refused to confess were hanged.

The first person to be executed was a young innkeeper named Bridget Bishop, who refused to say that she was a witch. She was publicly hanged from an oak tree on June 10, 1692.

The executions continued for the remainder of 1692 and into 1693. The victims were often elderly people. They were not permitted to be defended and were not allowed to have normal trials. Often, their bodies would be examined for unusual warts or other small growths, which the accusers said were used for suckling Satan's imps.

The Salem witch trials came to an end when people gradually realized that the accusations were the result of mass hysteria and lies. The tide turned against those who had carried out this persecution, and many, including the famous preacher Cotton Mather, were disgraced.

The Constitution and the Death Penalty

In 1789, six years after victory in the Revolution had established the independence of the 13 colonies, the Constitution was adopted. All the colonies had death-penalty laws at the time. But two of the Constitution's amendments referred to capital punishment in an indirect way only. These amendments do not state how capital punishment should apply or for what kinds of crimes it should be used.

The Fifth Amendment states: "No person shall be held to answer for a capital, or otherwise infamous crime, unless on a presentment or indictment of a Grand Jury . . . nor be deprived of life, liberty, or property, without due process of law . . . ."

The Eighth Amendment reads: "Excessive bail shall not be required, nor excessive fines imposed, nor cruel and unusual punishments inflicted." This phrase comes from the English Bill of Rights of 1689, which was adopted to stop extremely cruel forms of capital punishment, such as burning at the stake and beheading.

Prison Reform
in the 1800s
In the United States during the late 1700s and for most of the 1800s, the death penalty was imposed automatically for murder, treason, arson, and other serious crimes. Gradually, however, as the nation expanded westward and grew in population, many reform movements came into existence. One of these was the prison-reform movement, which started in the 1800s. In addition to improving the conditions within prisons, some reformers wanted the death penalty to be abolished. Although this goal was never achieved, many states gradually began to reject laws that *required* a death sentence for certain crimes. As part of this change, juries would have to decide separately and *after* a

person had been convicted whether he or she should be sentenced to death.

The U.S. Supreme Court was first asked to rule on whether the death penalty was "cruel and unusual punishment" in 1879. It ducked the issue. In a case called *Wilkerson* v. *Utah*, the Court allowed an execution by firing squad and said that only *certain kinds* of capital punishment, such as burning at the stake and beheading, were definitely cruel and unusual. But the Court ruled that it was not possible to say whether the death penalty by itself violated the Eighth Amendment.

Modern Methods of Execution

One of the results of the prison-reform movement was the invention of new and more modern ways of carrying out the death penalty. These new methods were thought to be quicker and more humane than hanging.

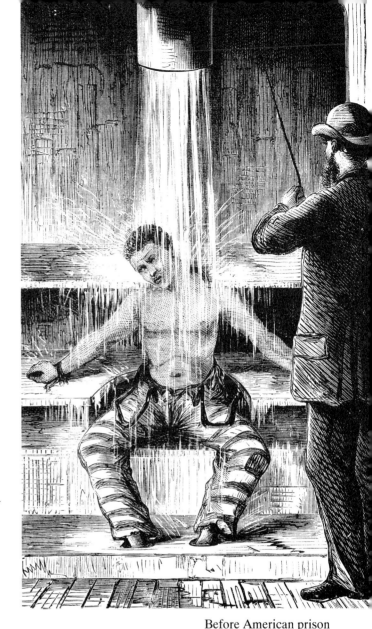

Before American prison reform in the 1800s, inmates were routinely tortured, abused, and even killed by authorities. The water torture, which often ended in death by exposure and exhaustion, was a popular method of punishment in New York's Sing Sing prison.

The major change was the invention of the electric chair, which was first used to execute someone in 1890. In 1888, the New York State legislature had passed a law that abolished hanging and replaced it with "death by electricity." A study done earlier by a special commission had discovered that most experts, including doctors, scientists, and judges, believed that death by electricity was more humane.

The decision to use electricity pitted two of the early pioneers of electric power against each other. Thomas Alva Edison favored its use for capital punishment, while George Westinghouse opposed it. Westinghouse was concerned that electricity, and his company, would get a bad name if they were associated with capital punishment.

Despite his strong opposition, Westinghouse's generator was used in 1890 to provide power for the first execution in an electric chair. The chair was invented by Edwin F. Davis, who would become the world's first electrical executioner.

The next new method of execution was death by lethal gas. In 1921, the state of Nevada passed a law abolishing capital punishment by hanging and the firing squad. In their place, death by gas was introduced.

Death by gas was thought to be a more humane improvement over the electric chair. In fact, under the Nevada law, the condemned person was not

Electricity pioneer, George Westinghouse, opposed the use of electricity for capital punishment.

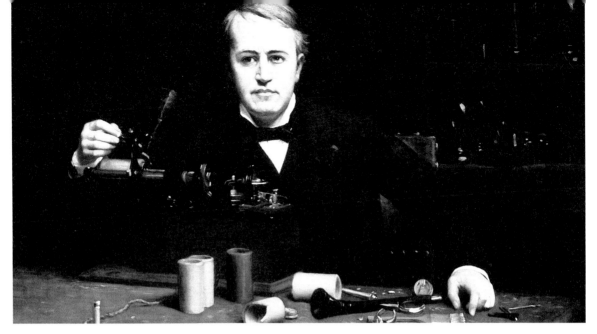

even supposed to know the date or hour of his or her own death. Gas would be pumped into the prison cell while the victim slept.

Thomas Alva Edison developed many uses for electrical power at his laboratory in Menlo Park, New Jersey. Edison approved of the idea of using electricity as a means of execution.

The plan, however, was dropped because it was impossible to build the necessary type of cell. Instead, a separate gas chamber was used—a small, airtight compartment in which the condemned person would sit strapped in a chair while poison gas was pumped into the chamber.

The first person to be executed by gas in the United States was Gee Jon, a Chinese immigrant convicted of murdering an elderly Chinese laundry-man. Gee Jon was executed in the gas chamber at Carson City, Nevada, on February 8, 1924.

Both the electric chair and the gas chamber are still in use today. The nation's most populous state, California, carries out capital-punishment sentences

"Old Sparky"

It was an ugly chair, but it was supposed to make things easier. It had broad arms, a high back, and thick leather straps dangling from it. There was also a headpiece and two wires that led to the two electrodes. The chair was attached to the floor, and it was insulated around its base.

And no one was quite certain how it would work when, on August 6, 1890, William Kemmler became the first person to sit down in it. The attention of the world was focused on the small upstate community of Auburn, New York. Outside the prison, it seemed as though the entire town had gathered to await the grim event.

Inside the prison, facing the chair, were 25 witnesses, including doctors, ministers, and the judge who had sentenced Kemmler. The prison warden, a man named Durston, was so nervous that he shook. The man who was the center of attention—who was about to make history—seemed the calmest one of all. He didn't want to make trouble. He just wanted it to go quickly.

Kemmler knew why he was there. The year before, when he was drunk, he had taken an axe and killed his girlfriend, Tillie, in the city of Buffalo, New York. Now he had to pay the price.

Early that morning, the hair on the top of Kemmler's head had been shaved away. Now, one of the electrodes was attached to the spot. The other electrode was placed at the base of his spine. Each electrode was made up of a rubber ball containing metal on the inside. The outside was covered with a wet sponge. These electrodes would carry the electricity quickly from the wire into the body. If it worked as it was supposed to, Kemmler would not know what hit him.

The headpiece, which partially hid the criminal's face, was put into position. A signal was given, and in the next room, a generator began humming.

Suddenly, Kemmler was rigid. If he had not been strapped into the chair, he might have been thrown clear across the room. The first jolt of electricity lasted 17 seconds. When

by using the gas chamber at San Quentin. One such execution at San Quentin occurred in the summer of 1992. Florida, the state that has performed the greatest number of executions in recent years, puts criminals to death in the electric chair at a prison near the city of Starke. The electric chairs and gas chambers in use today are not nearly as primitive as the first models used almost 70 years ago.

it stopped, Kemmler was examined by the doctors. He was still alive! The electricity was immediately turned on again. Smoke began to rise over the chair, and a sizzling sound filled the room.

After the second jolt, Kemmler was dead. The witnesses were shocked and appalled. Kemmler hadn't gone quickly. It had taken two jolts of electricity, and even with that, his body had been burned.

Over the years, executioners learned that people responded differently to electrical shock. What might kill one person might only stun another. Kemmler had received a relatively low voltage shock the first time. Now, an inmate receives a high-voltage shock for a few seconds, followed by a low-voltage shock for two or three more minutes.

In a way, the electric chair never overcame the image it received that August day in 1890. Because sparks often danced around the chairs during an execution, it received the name "Old Sparky," which is often used in prisons around the country.

Even though prisoners condemned to the electric chair and the gas chamber can now be assured of quick deaths, new technology has recently been invented in the hopes of making capital punishment even quicker and less painful. In 1977, Oklahoma decided not to spend money repairing its old electric chair. The idea of a gas chamber was also discarded because of the cost involved in building one from

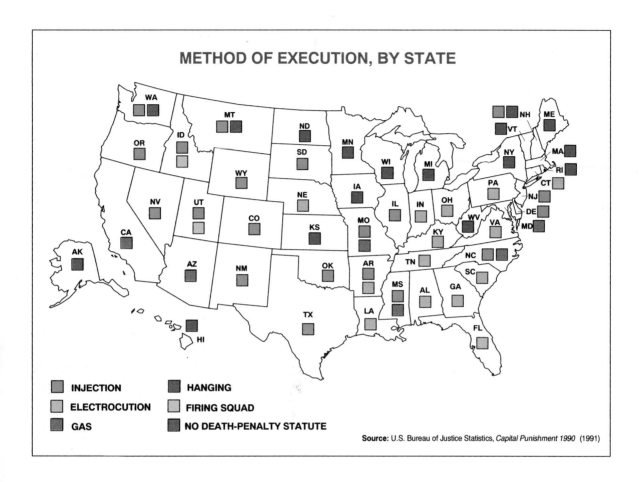

METHOD OF EXECUTION, BY STATE

LEGEND:
- INJECTION
- ELECTROCUTION
- GAS
- HANGING
- FIRING SQUAD
- NO DEATH-PENALTY STATUTE

Source: U.S. Bureau of Justice Statistics, *Capital Punishment 1990* (1991)

scratch. Instead, the state legislature passed a law calling for death by lethal injection.

Since Oklahoma first adopted death by the needle, 20 other states have followed. Lethal injection is now the main method of execution used in the United States. Some states still use the electric chair or the gas chamber. Fourteen states and the District of Columbia have no death-penalty statutes or have abolished the death penalty.

The Needle

When the electric chair was first used in 1890, people believed it would be a more humane form of execution than hanging. And, in 1924, when the gas chamber came into use, its advocates hoped it would be an advance over the electric chair. Both these forms of capital punishment had problems, however, at least when they were first used. So, in the late 1970s, a new method was created to carry out death-penalty sentences—death by lethal injection. Promoters of the needle believed it would be neat, clean, and painless.

Charles Brooks, Jr.

In this method of execution, the prisoner lies strapped to a gurney—a hospital cart. Three tubes are connected to his or her veins. One tube contains a sedative to put the prisoner to sleep, much in the way a doctor puts a patient under anesthesia for an operation. The second tube contains a poisonous substance that is injected after the person is unconscious. It causes the heart to stop. The third tube contains a harmless liquid. One person operates each of the tubes. Therefore, none of the three people knows who actually injected the poisonous liquid.

Arguments, however, soon developed over two issues. What role would doctors play in the administration of lethal injections, and what drugs would be used?

These were not easy questions to answer. The drugs approved for use by the Food and Drug Administration (FDA) in the United States are for healing people. One of the most important legal roles of the FDA is to monitor the safe use of all approved drugs. Could it legally stand aside as a drug meant to cure sick people was used by the government to kill people sentenced to death?

From the beginning, most doctors made it clear that they would have no part in giving deadly injections to inmates. In 1980, the American Medical Association (AMA) stated its position that a doctor's role is to heal, not to kill. The ability to give an injection is a learned skill. If a doctor would not take part, the risk of a botched execution was higher.

Both of these concerns became the basis for another legal challenge against the death penalty. In 1985, the U.S. Supreme Court ruled that the FDA did not have to exercise any role over the drugs used in an execution. The original suit had been filed by eight inmates who faced death by the needle.

Despite these problems, the needle soon became the preferred method for carrying out capital punishment. When offered the choice, almost all inmates sentenced to death chose lethal injection.

The first American who was executed by lethal injection was Charles Brooks, Jr. Convicted of murdering a used-car salesman whom he had robbed, he was put to death on December 7, 1982, in Fort Worth, Texas.

BUN
BBQ
Pardon
HELL!
I'll BRING
THE OIL TO
FRY HIM IN!!!
CHI-O CHI-O
IT'S OFF TO
HELL I GO!
THE
BUNDY-BBQ

3

The Debate About the Death Penalty

A crowd of about 300 people gathered outside the Raiford State Prison in Starke, Florida, just before dawn on January 24, 1989. Most of them were in a happy, partylike mood. They had come to await the electrocution of Ted Bundy, a 42-year-old man who had been convicted of the brutal murders of two young female students at the University of Florida and a 12-year-old girl from Lake City, Florida.

The crowd cheered and celebrated. Some carried signs that read "Burn, Bundy, Burn," "Thank God It's Fryday," and "Roast in Peace." Nearby, another group of people stood silently and prayed. They were opponents of the death penalty and had come to protest the taking of a human life by the state.

Hundreds of spectators gathered outside Raiford State Prison in Starke, Florida, in the early-morning hours of January 24, 1989, to celebrate the execution of murderer Ted Bundy.

Shortly after seven o'clock in the morning, a prison official came outside and told the crowd that Ted Bundy was dead. A loud cheer erupted, and firecrackers were lit in celebration. But many of the protesters wept.

Ted Bundy's case had drawn wide attention on television and in newspapers all over the country. Bundy was suspected of having killed as many as 50 women. Five books have been written about him, and a play was performed on television about his life. Bundy was a handsome and intelligent young man, and his face had become familiar to most Americans during the long years that his appeals went through the courts.

Ted Bundy was one of the worst mass murderers in American history. Good-looking and charming, many who knew him never suspected he was capable of such violence.

The scene outside the prison in Starke has been repeated many times outside other U.S. prisons. On the eve of an execution, crowds gather—one side expressing support for the death penalty, the other side opposing it. Although opinion polls say that the majority of Americans seem to want some form of the death penalty for murder, the issue of capital punishment is still very much alive.

Looking at the Legal Issues

As has already been noted, the U.S. Constitution refers to the death penalty but does not say how it should be carried out or for what crimes it should be used. It just assumes that it exists in law. For supporters of the death penalty, the mere fact that the Constitution refers to a death penalty is enough reason to retain it.

Since the beginning of the 1900s, however, the legal attack against the death penalty in the courts has been focused on the Eighth Amendment—the prohibition of "cruel and unusual punishment." In the Wilkerson case in 1879, the U.S. Supreme Court refused to say if capital punishment by itself was cruel and unusual. In 1890, the Court approved the use of electrocution in a case called *In re Kemmler.* This case was brought in response to the execution of William Kemmler, the first man to die in the electric chair. But the Court again refused to say if the death penalty by itself—regardless of why it was imposed or how it was carried out—was unconstitutional.

It was not until 1972 that the Supreme Court spoke on the death penalty in relation to the Eighth Amendment. The case was *Furman* v. *Georgia*. In its decision, the Court struck down the laws of Georgia and Texas that—like many others in the country—allowed juries to impose the death sentence on a convicted criminal. The Court said that because the juries received inadequate guidance and because the jury systems differed so much from state to state, the death penalty as applied under these situations was cruel and unusual punishment.

For the next four years, there were no executions in the United States. Many states rewrote their death-penalty laws. In 1976, in *Gregg* v. *Georgia*, the Supreme Court ruled that the rewritten laws of a number of states were constitutional.

What the states had done was to rewrite their laws in such a way that the death penalty would be imposed by juries under the careful guidance of the trial court. The Supreme Court stated that the Eighth Amendment also allows state legislatures to impose the death penalty. The Court had finally spoken: As long as it is administered fairly, the death penalty by itself is *not* cruel and unusual punishment.

The Supreme Court on the Death Penalty Since 1976

With its decision in the *Gregg* v. *Georgia* case in 1976, the U.S. Supreme Court ruled that the death penalty by itself is not cruel and unusual punishment. Since then, the Court has been asked to rule on a number of issues having to do with how capital punishment is applied. Among the major cases since 1976 are the following:

Coker v. *Georgia* (1977): The Court ruled that a Georgia law authorizing capital punishment in certain cases of rape violates the Eighth Amendment prohibition of cruel and unusual punishment because it is disproportionate to the crime.

Enmund v. *Florida* (1982): The Court ruled that imposing the death penalty on someone who aided in a felony that resulted in a murder, but who did not do the killing, violated the Eighth Amendment.

Pulley v. *Harris* (1984): The Court ruled that the Eighth Amendment does not require that lower courts compare a death sentence with earlier sentences for similar crimes in order to see if the punishment is appropriate.

Spaziano v. *Florida* (1984): The Court ruled that a judge may overrule a jury's recommendation for life in prison but may not overrule the jury and impose a death sentence.

Turner v. *Murray* (1986): The Court ruled that a defendant facing a death sentence has the right to have jurors told the race of the crime victim. The defendant also has the right to question possible jurors about racial bias.

Ford v. *Wainwright* (1986): The Court ruled that the Eighth Amendment prohibits states from executing criminals judged to be insane.

McCleskey v. *Kemp* (1987): The Court ruled that statistics showing that more blacks are executed than whites do not prove that defendants' rights have been violated. A defendant needs to prove that the decision makers in the case intentionally intended to discriminate before he or she can claim a violation under the Eighth Amendment.

Penry v. *Lynaugh* (1989): The Court ruled that the Eighth Amendment does not prohibit the execution of a person who has been diagnosed as mentally retarded.

Does the Death Penalty Reduce Crime?

Another area of debate concerning the death penalty is whether it actually helps reduce crime.

Those in favor of the death penalty believe that it deters crime. That is, the very knowledge that a person faces death will make that individual think twice before committing a serious crime.

Those opposed to the death penalty disagree. They point to the fact that, while the United States has death-penalty laws in 36 states, the country has one of the highest murder rates in the world. In contrast, Great Britain, which abolished the death penalty in 1969 for all crimes except high treason and piracy with violence (skyjacking),

Police officers arrest a group of suspects believed to be part of a drug operation in Los Angeles. California still has a death-penalty law but has not executed anyone in more than 20 years.

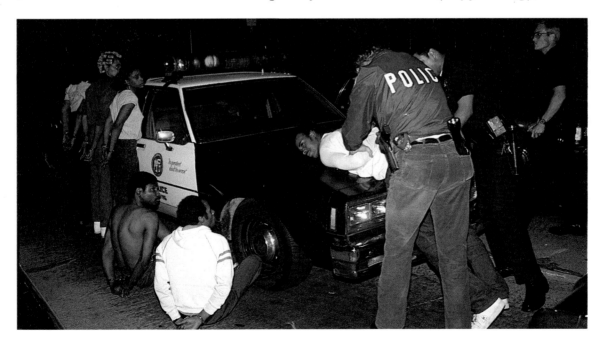

has one of the lowest murder rates in the world. If the threat of the death penalty reduces violent crime, why does the United States have such a high murder rate?

The argument over whether the death penalty does or does not deter crime has gone on for years and is likely to continue. A June 1992 Gallup Poll survey showed that most Americans still believe that it is better to have some kind of death-penalty laws than to abolish them altogether.

Can We Afford the Death Penalty?

Both those in favor of capital punishment and those opposed to it have raised one very practical question: Can states afford to administer the death penalty?

Those who favor the death penalty argue that it is more costly to keep a criminal in prison for life than it is to execute him or her.

Opponents of capital punishment say that lengthy legal appeals and the cost of keeping death-penalty equipment in condition place a heavy financial burden on states. Their argument, however, has made little headway in state legislatures. Most of the legislators and governors are concerned with prison reform in general, because the court system is clogged with cases, and most of the country's prisons are filled to capacity.

The death-penalty debate has stilled somewhat in the early 1990s. The Supreme Court has ruled that capital punishment is not cruel and unusual. And the American people, according to national surveys, seem to want to have some death-penalty laws. Prison reform in general has become a much larger political issue, which focuses more on preventing crime, on rehabilitating criminals, and on improving methods for housing America's prisoners.

PRISON FACTS AT A GLANCE

	1971	1991
Prison and jail inmates	359,000	1,150,000
Prisoners per 100,000 population	96	293
Inmates on death row	642	2,400
Reported serious crimes per 100,000 population	4,165	5,820
Number of states under court order to improve prison conditions	Not available	41

	1984	1991
Inmate homicides	118	56
Inmate suicides	114	101
Inmate escapes	7,903	7,244

1990 average prison operating cost: $18,000 per inmate.

Source: U.S. Bureau of Justice Statistics, *Corrections Compendium*, Corrections Yearbook, ACLU Prison Project

Life on Death Row

Imagine yourself living in a room 12 feet long by 6 feet wide. In this room you have only a bed, a table and chair, a sink, and a toilet bowl. Most likely, there is no window. You spend the majority of your time in this room. You eat all your meals in this room. You go to the bathroom in this room. You can exercise, and you are allowed to read and write letters in this room. You cannot have visitors. For that, you must go somewhere else, where you will be watched constantly and where your visitor will probably have to sit behind a mesh screen.

Once a week, you are allowed to leave the room to take a shower. Your days can be long and boring. You spend them reading, thinking, and worrying—especially worrying. You are not in any ordinary room. You are in a cell on "death row," a part of the prison that is reserved for people who have been sentenced to die for committing terrible and violent crimes against other human beings.

Depending on what state you're in, death will be by the electric chair, by lethal injection, or in a gas chamber. But, chances are, death will not come for years and years. After conviction, your defense lawyers will begin the lengthy appeal procedure of taking your case to the lower courts and then, if necessary, to the U.S. Supreme Court and the governor of the state.

If all appeals fail, and the dreaded day comes, the prisoner is moved to a holding cell the day before execution. A holding cell is a small room near the room in which the execution will take place. There, the prisoner is offered a last meal of any food. Some prisoners have chosen snack foods or pizza, while others have asked for large meals. Many are too nervous to eat at all. The inmate's last visitors are likely to be his or her lawyer, family members, and a prison chaplain who offers to pray with the prisoner.

The last walk to the death chamber takes place in the company of guards and the warden, whose job is to read the sentence of death to the condemned criminal. A few invited witnesses—prison officials, sometimes a close friend, and selected members of the press—are present to watch the execution.

In a matter of moments, it's over.

Can We Be The Judge?

Since the founding of our country, about 8,000 people have been legally executed. Have people been wrongfully put to death? Many people sentenced to death have proclaimed their innocence to the end, but were any *really* innocent?

It is painful to think about an innocent person going to the electric chair or the gas chamber. But it has happened. Opponents of the death penalty often cite the risk of executing innocent people as a good enough reason to abolish the death penalty. Better that a guilty person should go free, they say, than an innocent one die. Those in favor of the death penalty will point out that mistakes—even dreadful mistakes—can happen, but that the good of society as a whole is what counts in the end. A patient may die while having a simple operation, but we don't then abolish surgery, they say.

One of the most notorious cases in American history was the trial and execution of Nicola Sacco and Bartolomeo Vanzetti, two Italian immigrants who went to the electric chair in Massachusetts in 1927. Sacco and Vanzetti were arrested and tried for murdering two bank officials during a robbery in 1920. Throughout their trial, the evidence linking them to the crime was extremely weak.

But it was only a few years after World War I, and the country was in an antiforeign mood. Sacco and Vanzetti were seen as violent "foreigners." They were sentenced to die.

In the years that Sacco and Vanzetti sat on death row, their case became known around the world. Prominent people from all walks of life called for a new trial. A commission appointed by the governor of Massachusetts reviewed the evidence and decided that Sacco and Vanzetti had received a fair trial.

Bartolomeo Vanzetti (*right*) and Nicola Sacco (*middle*) leave court escorted by armed guards after being sentenced to death by electrocution.

On August 23, 1927, they were executed. When their bodies were released to the funeral home, thousands of people marched in the streets. News of their death set off riots in cities across the United States. American embassies in foreign countries were attacked.

Were Sacco and Vanzetti innocent? Probably. But many books have been written arguing both sides of the question. The point is that a large segment of the population *believed* they were the innocent victims of antiforeign prejudice.

In 1977, Massachusetts governor Michael Dukakis pardoned Sacco and Vanzetti, declaring them to be innocent "forever." The fiftieth anniversary of their execution was declared a holiday in Massachusetts.

The Rosenbergs:
The Death Penalty for Spying

Ethel Rosenberg (*left*), Deputy Marshal Harry McCabe (*center*), and Julius Rosenberg (*right*).

Julius and Ethel Rosenberg were an average-looking couple in their thirties. They lived in New York City and had two young sons. Julius was an electrical engineer, and Ethel was a housewife.

On June 19, 1953, the Rosenbergs were executed in the electric chair at Sing Sing prison in New York for giving away data on the atomic bomb to the USSR. They were the only Americans ever executed in peacetime for spying and high treason.

Despite appearances, the Rosenbergs led secret lives. A member of the Communist party, Julius was often in contact with Soviet agents, and Ethel sometimes helped him.

In 1944, Ethel's brother, David Greenglass, was working on the atomic bomb for the U.S. Army. Julius persuaded Greenglass to give him information about the bomb, which Julius then passed on to Soviet agents.

In 1950, the Rosenbergs were arrested by U.S. agents and charged with espionage (spying). Greenglass testified against Julius and Ethel, who refused to admit their guilt. After a highly publicized trial, they were convicted in 1951 and sentenced to death.

In imposing such a severe sentence, Judge Irving Kaufman stated that the Rosenbergs had threatened world peace and endangered the lives of millions. Because of their spying, the Soviet Union had nuclear weapons.

For two years, the Rosenbergs waged a powerful struggle to avoid the death penalty. At one point, the pope even pleaded for them. President Dwight Eisenhower turned down five separate pleas for presidential clemency.

The Rosenberg case won't go away. Books are still being written debating the couple's guilt or innocence and the appropriateness of their sentence. The evidence brought out at the trial shows that Julius *did* pass some kind of information on to the Soviet Union. But how important could it have been in the development of the bomb? Most scientists now agree that the Soviets were well on their way to developing a bomb on their own. It is unlikely that anything the Rosenbergs passed on could have been that important.

A number of military people were tried for espionage in the 1980s. They had passed secrets on to the USSR, and in one case, to Israel. All received long prison sentences. Espionage is still a serious crime, but in no case since the Rosenberg execution has the death penalty been imposed.

The claim of innocence continues to have a powerful impact when it comes from a condemned person. In May 1992, a young Virginia man named Roger Keith Coleman was electrocuted for the rape and murder of his sister-in-law. He had insisted on his innocence from the beginning, and a number of prominent lawyers and ministers took up his case. A few weeks before his execution, his picture appeared on *Time* magazine's cover.

As with Sacco and Vanzetti, the evidence in the Roger Keith Coleman case was considered weak. No one had seen Coleman commit the crime, and other evidence was strongly challenged.

The Supreme Court and the governor of Virginia, however, felt that justice had been served. Roger Keith Coleman joined a long list of defendants whose last words were, "I am innocent."

In a case pending before the Supreme Court, a death-row inmate in Texas named Leonel Herrera, who was convicted of killing two police officers in 1981, claims that he is innocent and is asking the justices to consider new evidence that casts his conviction in doubt. At issue is whether federal courts can hear a prisoner's claim that he is not guilty. In the past, federal courts have considered only whether there were procedural errors in the original trial. In other words, is innocence enough to overturn a death sentence?

Women and the Death Penalty

Margie Velma Barfield, a 52-year-old grandmother, was an unlikely candidate for the death penalty. Yet, in the early morning hours of November 2, 1984, she was strapped to a gurney in a room at Central Prison in Raleigh, North Carolina, and became the first woman in the United States to die by lethal injection.

Margie Barfield

Margie Barfield had a problem with drugs prescribed by her doctors. She had become addicted to tranquilizers, sleeping pills, and a number of other medications. In order to get money to pay for her drugs, she stole from friends and family. In 1978, she forged her boyfriend's name on a check. Afraid that she would be discovered, Margie mixed rat poison into his beer and went off to church. An autopsy revealed that he had been poisoned, and Barfield was arrested.

Barfield confessed that she had poisoned her mother, had given roach poison to her second husband, and had killed two elderly people she was taking care of—all because she was afraid of being discovered as a thief. She claimed that she never meant to kill anyone and that her mind was clouded by drugs when she committed all these crimes. But she was sentenced to death and accepted the verdict.

Barfield's case drew national attention. The idea of executing a woman—and in this case a grandmother—made people uncomfortable. No woman had been executed in the United States since 1962. The appeals for mercy in Barfield's case were widespread, and in vain. When it was clear that her time had run out, Barfield ordered a last meal of Cheez Doodles and a Coke and put on pink pajamas for her execution. She apologized for her crimes and went peacefully to her death. To make amends, she donated her body to a hospital so her organs might be used for people needing transplants.

Only .02 percent of the people on death row are women. More men commit violent crimes, so fewer women are sentenced to death. But whenever a woman is sentenced to death, it arouses national interest.

The first woman to die in the electric chair was Martha Place, executed in New York State on March 20, 1899, for the axe murder of her 17-year-old stepdaughter. The Place execution caused great concern for Governor Theodore Roosevelt, who was reluctant to put a woman to death. After consulting with doctors, lawyers, and judges, he ordered the execution and allowed that only women attend Place in her final moments.

One of the most riveting executions of a woman occurred at Sing Sing, in New York State, on January 12, 1928. Ruth Snyder, a housewife from Queens, New York, was electrocuted for murdering her husband to collect on his life-insurance policy. Snyder was tried along with her boyfriend, who had helped her with the murder, and both were sentenced to death. A newspaper reporter who was invited to witness the execution had secretly strapped a camera to his leg. At the moment the current surged through Ruth Snyder's body, he snapped the shutter.

The next day, the front page of the *New York Daily News* contained a full-page photo of Ruth Snyder at the moment that she was executed. People were horrified that such a picture could be taken. But the enormous interest in any woman condemned to death continued—and continues to the present.

No woman has been executed in the United States since Margie Velma Barfield was put to death in 1984.

Ruth Snyder

Update: The Death Penalty Today

From the time of Gary Gilmore's execution in 1977 until the autumn of 1992, 181 people were executed for murder in the United States. The rate of execution today is much lower than it was 50 years ago. In 1935, for example, 199 people were executed, the highest annual rate ever. As of 1992, more than 2,000 people were sitting in cells on death row.

The likelihood of somcone being sentenced to death depends totally on where he or she lives. If you commit premeditated murder in New York—that is, if you carry out a murder you planned in advance—the longest sentence you will receive is 25 years to life imprisonment. The only situation in which the death penalty is handed down in New York is when a law-enforcement official is murdered.

Executions have become highly publicized and hotly debated events in America. Today, an execution is an important event for newpapers, magazines, and television news coverage.

If you commit premeditated murder in Louisiana, North Carolina, or Oklahoma and are convicted, you will receive the death penalty automatically— without exception. If you are sentenced to death in Florida or Texas, you have a very strong chance of being executed. Florida and Texas have executed the greatest number of people since 1976.

Since the reinstatement of the death penalty in 1976, only 13 of the 36 states with death-penalty laws have actually executed criminals. No matter where you live, the appeals process will take from 7 to 11 years, depending on the case and the work-load of the court system at all levels.

Current Attitudes
About the Death Penalty
Traditionally, there has been a high level of support in the United States for the death penalty. Gallup Poll surveys show that support was weakest during the 1960s but that it rose again during the 1970s and 1980s and today remains relatively high.

According to this poll, approximately 53 percent of Americans of all races believe that the death penalty is an effective deterrent in reducing crime.

Over the period from 1936 through 1991, the Gallup Poll asked a cross section of Americans if there should be a death penalty for the crime of murder. In the period from 1966 to 1988, support

The Death Penalty in the Military

The U.S. federal and state governments are not the only jurisdictions that can impose the death penalty for crimes. The military also has the power to sentence people to death.

When men and women join the army, navy, air force, or marines, they are judged under military law. Although military law must conform to the basic principles of the U.S. Constitution, it differs in a number of ways.

A military case is not tried by a jury, but by a court-martial, a panel of officers selected to hear the case. The military may sentence people to death for the same kinds of crimes committed in civilian life, but it may also impose the death penalty for desertion in time of war. It has carried out executions both by hanging and by firing squad.

In peacetime, the military rarely carries out executions. Today, if a member of the armed forces committed murder, he or she would most likely be prosecuted by civilian authorities.

The last execution for desertion that was conducted by the U.S. military took place in Europe in 1945, during the final days of World War II. Eddie Slovik, a 25-year-old private from Detroit, Michigan, was so afraid of combat that he deserted from his unit twice. Slovik made the mistake of saying that he would desert his unit again if he could. Many soldiers had deserted during the war, and all of them had been imprisoned. When it was discovered that Slovik had a criminal record in civilian life, the military decided to make an example of him.

The military sentenced Eddie Slovik to die by firing squad. A last-minute appeal to the supreme Allied commander, General Dwight Eisenhower, was rejected, and Slovik was shot by a firing squad made up of 12 men from his unit. He was buried in an American military cemetery near Château Thierry, France.

After his death, Slovik's widow, Antoinette, tried to collect his military life-insurance policy. Because her husband had been executed, she was denied the money. But she kept up the fight, all the time believing an injustice had been committed against her husband. In 1978, President Jimmy Carter sponsored a bill in Congress to pay Antoinette Slovik the $70,000 from the life-insurance policy. She died, however, before Congress could act on the bill. Eddie Slovik's remains were removed from the cemetery in France and taken to Detroit in 1987.

In World War II, 100 men were executed by the military, all for having murdered or raped civilians. One—Eddie Slovik—was executed for desertion.

THE DEATH PENALTY AT A GLANCE

SUPPORT FOR CAPITAL PUNISHMENT

Number of Americans in favor of the death penalty   1966: 42%   1990: 79%

- Percentage of Americans who believe the death penalty deters crime: 53%
- Percentage of Americans who believe more executions are the best way to reduce crime: 33%
- Percentage of Americans who believe more crime-prevention measures are the best way to reduce crime: 65%

CAPITAL PUNISHMENT AND RACE

Throughout the history of capital punishment, there have been more whites executed than blacks. As a percentage of their relative populations, however, more blacks per capita are sentenced to death.

- Between 1930 and 1939, 803 whites and 687 blacks were executed in the United States. Only 30 of those people were women (18 whites and 12 blacks). Twenty years later, between 1950 and 1959, the proportion of whites to blacks executed remained the same. During that period, 316 whites and 280 blacks were executed for the crime of murder.

- Between 1976 and 1992, there were 181 people executed in the United States. About 60% of those people were nonwhite (blacks and other minorities).

- Percentage of African Americans who believe the death penalty deters crime: 47%

Source: *The 1992 World Almanac*; U S. Bureau of Justice Statistics (*Sourcebook of Criminal Justice Statistics*).

for the death penalty almost doubled, going from 42 percent to 79 percent. What is the meaning of such a change? The experts believe that several factors are responsible for this attitude. For one, the nation's attitudes toward capital punishment became more strict during this time. Second, the crime rate for all crimes rose dramatically between the 1960s and the 1980s. Increased support for the death penalty coincided with the belief that all criminals should be treated more harshly than the courts were treating them.

Few criminologists believe these figures are likely to change dramatically in the near future.

What Does the Future Hold?

The current Supreme Court has a majority of members appointed by Ronald Reagan and George Bush—both conservatives. These conservative justices show little sign of overturning the death penalty. In fact, the rulings of the last 12 years indicate that the death penalty is fairly safe from attack on the federal-court level.

Increasingly, opponents have turned to the state legislatures for change. But even here the battle has tilted in favor of supporters of capital punishment. In New York State, however, Mario Cuomo, who became governor in 1983, is a staunch opponent of capital punishment. He says that he will never allow anyone to be executed while he is in office.

Every year since Cuomo became governor, the New York legislature has passed a bill reinstating

New York governor Mario Cuomo (*left*) answers questions at a press conference with New York City mayor David Dinkins (*right*). Cuomo strongly opposes capital punishment and has worked to keep death-penalty proposals from becoming law in New York.

the death penalty for premeditated murder. Every year, Governor Cuomo has vetoed the bill, and the legislature has failed to override his veto. Each year, the vote has become closer and closer. In 1991, the legislature almost overrode the veto. In both houses many were in favor of restoring the death penalty, but a two-thirds majority is needed to override. Supporters of the death penalty fell short by only a few votes.

In other states without the death penalty there is also pressure on the state legislatures to restore capital punishment. In the meantime, the appeals process continues to take years and years, and in this lengthy period lies hope for many of those convicted. There is always a chance that, in the end, perhaps a governor will grant a reprieve.

A recent execution in the United States—on September 16, 1992—took place in the state of Virginia. The governor, L. Douglas Wilder, a black man, refused to pardon the condemned man. In prison was Willie Leroy Jones, a 34-year-old black man convicted of murdering an elderly couple in 1983. After shooting them, he threw the woman's body into a closet and set the house on fire. The motive was robbery. After stealing $30,000 from the couple, Jones fled to Hawaii and went on a spending spree. He was captured there and returned to Virginia.

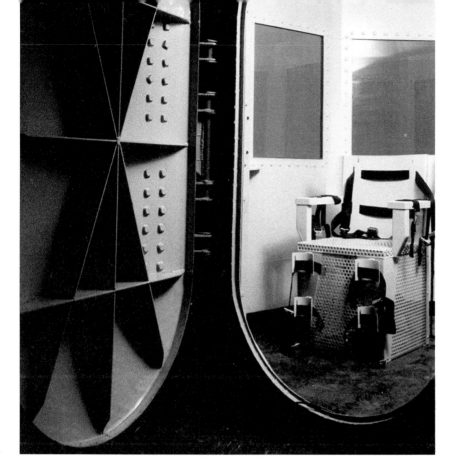

Executions in California, the most populous state in the nation, are carried out in this gas chamber at San Quentin prison. The debate over capital punishment in America will continue for as long as people try to decide if state-sponsored death can really be called justice.

Jones's appeals had taken nine years and four months. As he was strapped into the electric chair at the Greensville Correctional Center, he said, "Killing me is not the answer. There is a place called prison."

The sister of the man Jones had murdered agreed. "I don't believe in capital punishment," she said, after Jones was electrocuted.

A majority of Americans, however, believe that capital punishment *is* an answer to violent crime. As long as this attitude prevails, the United States is likely to have a death penalty.

Glossary

appeal A legal procedure that attempts to get a lower-court decision overturned by taking the case to a higher court.

auto-da-fé A ritual mass burning at the stake during the Spanish Inquisition.

Bill of Rights The first 10 amendments to the U.S. Constitution.

capital punishment The death sentence.

court-martial A military trial, conducted by a panel of officers.

crucifixion In Roman times, a death sentence carried out by hanging a person from a cross to which the hands and feet have been nailed or tied.

Eighth Amendment In the Bill of Rights, the amendment that prohibits cruel and unusual punishment.

electrocution A form of the death penalty carried out by strapping a person in a chair and killing him or her with electric shocks.

espionage The crime of spying for another country.

execution The action of putting a criminal to death.

Fifth Amendment In the Bill of Rights, the amendment that guarantees due process of law for persons accused of committing crimes.

gas chamber An airtight room used to execute criminals by means of poison gas.

guillotine A device used to behead people, which was made famous during the French Revolution.

heresy Doctrines and beliefs that are opposed by an organized religion.

Inquisition A Roman Catholic court that was set up to prosecute people who were accused of opposing religious beliefs.

lethal injection A form of the death penalty carried out by injecting fatal amounts of drugs into a person's veins.

premeditated murder Murder that is planned; the most severely punished degree of murder.

religious persecution The act of attacking or harming people because of their religious beliefs.

treason The betrayal of one's country to a foreign power.

For Further Reading

Brown, Gene. *Violence on America's Streets.* Brookfield, CT: The Millbrook Press, 1992.

Hays, S. *Capital Punishment.* Vero Beach, FL: Rourke Publishing, 1990.

Kent, Zachary. *The Story of the Salem Witch Trials* (Cornerstones of Freedom Series). New York: Childrens Press, 1986.

Lawrence, John. *The History of Capital Punishment.* New York: Citadel Press, 1983.

Rickard, Graham. *Prisons and Punishment.* New York: Franklin Watts, 1987.

Robins, Dave. *Just Punishment.* New York: Franklin Watts, 1990.

Source Notes

Abelson,Raziel, and Friquegnon, Marie-Louise, eds. *Ethics for Modern Life,* 4th ed., New York: St. Martin's Press, 1991.

Bedau, Hugo. *The Death Penalty in America*, 3d. ed. New York: Oxford University Press, 1982.

Drimmer, Frederick. *Until You Are Dead. . . The Book of Executions in America.* New York: Citadel Press, 1990.

Gallup Poll Quarterly, June 1992.

Norman Mailer, *The Executioner's Song,* 1979.

Joyce, James. *Capital Punishment: A World View* (Capital Punishment Series), reprint. New York: AMS Press, 1967.

Leeson, Susan M., and Foster, James C. *American Constitutional Law: Cases in Context.* New York: St. Martin's Press, 1992.

The New Columbia Encyclopedia (articles on historical figures; "capital punishment."), 1975.

Statistical Abstract of the United States (various years).

"Virginia Executes Man Convicted in Rape Murder." *The New York Times,* July 25, 1992.

Index

Photo Credits

Cover: ©John Chiasson/Gamma-Liaison; pp. 5, 7, 30, 35, 36–37, 38, 42, 47, 48, 50, 51, 52–53, 57, 59: AP/Wide World Photos; pp. 10–11, 12, 13, 15, 16, 17, 18, 19, 20, 22–23, 26, 29: North Wind Photo Archives; pp. 31, 41, 55: Blackbirch Photo Archives; p.33: ©John Chiasson/Gamma-Liaison. Maps and charts by Sandra Burr.